For Billy and Michelle
and Denise, Louise, and Nic

First U.S. edition 2011

Library of Congress Cataloging-in-Publication Data
Ross, Fiona, date.
Chilly Milly Moo / Fiona Ross. —1st U.S. ed.
p.   cm.
Summary: While the other cows are enjoying the sun and making plenty of milk, Milly Moo is too hot to make a drop but when the
temperature falls, Milly Moo shows the farmer and the rest of the herd what she can do.
ISBN 978-0-7636-5693-5
[1. Cows—Fiction. 2. Individuality—Fiction. 3. Milking—Fiction. 4. Weather—Fiction.]   I. Title.
PZ7.R19648Chi 2011
[E]—dc22   2010051446

11 12 13 14 15 16 SCP 10 9 8 7 6 5 4 3 2

Printed in Humen, Dongguan, China

This book was typeset in WB Fiona Ross. The illustrations were created digitally.

Candlewick Press, 99 Dover Street, Somerville, Massachusetts 02144

visit us at www.candlewick.com

Chilly Milly Moo

Fiona Ross

CANDLEWICK PRESS

Milly Moo the cow was sad.
"What's up?" mooed the other cows.

Milly Moo the cow was glum.

"What's up?" asked the farmer.

It's too hot for me to make milk.

Milly Moo wanted to churn out the finest, loveliest, tastiest, creamiest milk.

But she couldn't.

"You can't stay here if you can't make milk," said the farmer.

"Aw, what a poor cow! We make lots of milk," boasted the others.

The other cows snickered. They couldn't understand why Milly Moo was different.

That night Milly Moo
dreamed about what might
happen to her.

Where did cows
that couldn't
make milk
go?

She woke to find that a storm was raging.

It was getting colder.

The farmer came to collect the milk.

"This is your last chance, Milly Moo," he said.

The farmer squeezed and squeezed and squeezed...

GURGLE
GARGLE

"Let's have one last try!"

Strange noises erupted from Milly Moo.

BUBBLE BABBLE

"Blimey!"
said the farmer.

And there was an explosion
of the coldest, chilliest,
frostiest, iciest . . .

The other cows
wished that they could
be like Milly Moo.

We can't make ice cream!

"Don't be misery moos," said Milly Moo.

"We're all special!"
said Milly Moo.
"It's just that I like being chilly.
Let's go and enjoy the big freeze!"

And they did.